A GOLDEN BOOK • NEW YORK

randomhouse.com/kids

ISBN 978-0-7364-3260-3

MANUFACTURED IN CHINA

10 9 8 7

a Little Golden Book® Collection

Disney

Nine Classic Tales

A GOLDEN BOOK · NEW YORK

CONTENTS

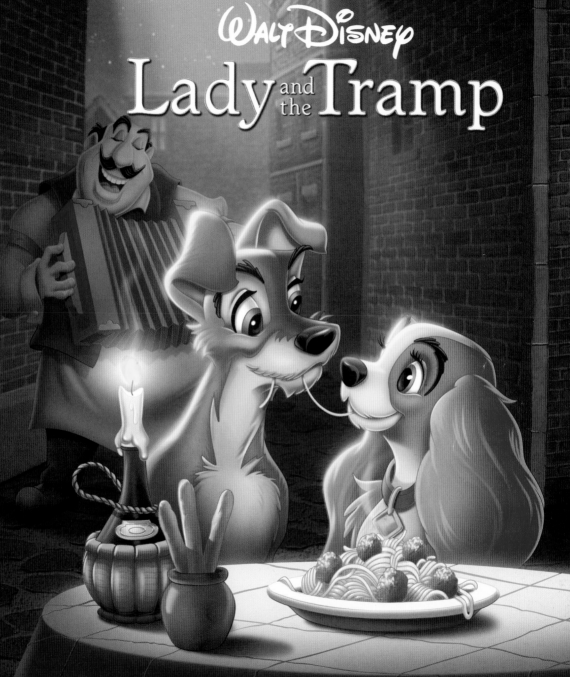

Lady was a lucky little cocker spaniel. She had everything a dog could want. Her beloved owners, Jim Dear and Darling, had pampered her since puppyhood. They gave her the tastiest tidbits to eat and the softest bed to sleep in, and they showered her with affection.

Lady returned this kindness by waking her master each morning with a gentle lick on the cheek. And while he was at work, Lady stayed close to her mistress, protecting her from possible harm.

But one day, everything changed. As Lady told her friends, Trusty and Jock, Darling now seemed more interested in the tiny sweater she was knitting than in her faithful friend.

Lady's pals quickly put two and two together and figured out that Darling was going to have a baby.

"Babies are mighty sweet," Trusty the bloodhound said.

"And very, very soft," Jock the Scottie added. "Why, a wee babe is nothin' but a bundle of—"

"—trouble!" an unfamiliar voice chimed in.

The voice belonged to a scruffy stranger named Tramp. Though Tramp had no family of his own, he seemed to know quite a lot about babies—and none of it was good.

"Take it from me, Pigeon," Tramp told Lady. "A human heart has only so much room for love and affection. When a baby moves in, the dog moves out!"

Although Tramp's words worried Lady, she couldn't believe that her family would ever be unkind. And once the baby was born, Lady saw just how wrong Tramp had been. For not only did Lady still have her family's love, she now had one more person to cherish and protect.

Everything was fine until Jim Dear and Darling decided to take a short vacation.

"Don't worry, old girl," Jim Dear told Lady before they left. "Aunt Sarah will be staying here to care for you and the baby."

But Aunt Sarah soon made it clear that she did not
like dogs at all. To make matters worse, she had brought
her two nasty cats along. Lady watched helplessly as
they wrecked the living room and terrorized the goldfish
and the bird.

When the cats headed upstairs, however, Lady
sprang into action. She raced ahead to stop them from
entering the nursery. The nasty creatures tried to run by
her, but Lady stopped them in their tracks with a
threatening growl.

Aunt Sarah heard the commotion and poked her head out of the nursery. She took one look at Lady growling and the two cats sniveling, and she ran to protect her pets.

"Oh, my precious pusses," she crooned. And scooping the cats up in her arms, she carried them gently downstairs.

Then Aunt Sarah dragged Lady off to the pet store.
"I want a muzzle for this vicious beast," she told the salesclerk.
"I have just the thing," the clerk replied, placing one of
the awful contraptions over the struggling dog's face.
In desperation, poor Lady ran out of the store.

Outside, a pack of stray dogs began to chase her.
Horns blared and tires screeched as Lady raced blindly
through the streets, across the railroad tracks, and into a
strange and scary part of town.

Her heart pounding, Lady ran on with the strays
yapping at her heels. Just when she felt she couldn't take
another step, a brown ball of fur rushed to her side.

Biting and barking, Tramp fought off Lady's attackers
until every last one had turned tail and slunk away.

Tramp helped Lady remove the hateful muzzle, and then she told him her tale of woe.

"Poor Pidge," he said when she had finished her story. "You sure have had a terrible day. What you need is a night out on the town to cheer you up!"

Tramp led Lady to a quaint little Italian restaurant.
There they shared a delicious plate of spaghetti and
meatballs while musicians serenaded them with a
romantic tune.

After dinner, Lady and Tramp took a moonlight stroll. When they came to a patch of wet cement, Tramp scratched a big heart in the middle and placed one of his paws inside it. Lady did the same.

A silvery moon was high in the sky when the two tired dogs finally snuggled up under a tree and fell fast asleep.

When they awoke the next morning, Lady was horrified to realize she had spent the whole night away from home.

"Aw, Pidge," Tramp said, "there's a big wide world out there just waiting for us. Why go back at all?"

"Because my family needs me," Lady replied. "And I need them. Besides, who will protect the baby if I'm not there?"

Tramp had no answer for that. He simply bowed his head in defeat. And even though Lady was sad to leave Tramp, she could hardly wait to return to her family.

But when Lady got home, an angry Aunt Sarah was waiting for her. "I have a special place for you now," Aunt Sarah snapped as she led Lady to a doghouse in the backyard. "This should keep you out of trouble!" she said, chaining Lady to a stake in the ground.

That night Lady was moping around the yard when a
big gray rat scurried out of the woodpile, scampered up
the porch railing, and darted into an upstairs window.

"That's the baby's room!" Lady cried. She dashed
forward but was jerked to a painful halt by her chain.
Lady barked frantically to attract Aunt Sarah's attention.

Aunt Sarah finally appeared at the back door, but only to yell at Lady. "Stop that racket!" she said before slamming the door again.

Just then, Tramp raced into the yard. He had heard Lady barking and had come to help her once more.

"There's a rat in the baby's room!" Lady said. And with no thought for his own safety, Tramp ran inside to get the rat.

Tramp reached the nursery in the nick of time. The baby lay sleeping in the crib, and the rat was ready to pounce.

Tramp struck first. Fur flew and furniture fell as dog and rat tore around the room. The rat was fast and fierce, but he was no match for Tramp.

By the time Aunt Sarah burst in, there was no sign of the rat—just Tramp and the topsy-turvy room. Aunt Sarah thought that Tramp had been after the baby, and she quickly called the dogcatcher.

"Don't come back, you vicious brute," Aunt Sarah warned as Tramp was carried off to the pound.

As soon as Lady explained what had happened,
Trusty and Jock took off after Tramp. They chased the
dogcatcher through the dark and stormy night.

When a taxi appeared out of the fog, the dogcatcher's
horses reared up and his wagon toppled over. Jim Dear
and Darling were in the taxi. They had come home and
discovered the rat. It was clear then that Tramp had been
protecting the baby, and they went after him. He was a
true hero!

Jim Dear and Darling decided to take Tramp into their home.

"This is where you belong," Jim Dear told Tramp. "You're part of our family now."

And soon Lady and Tramp had a family of their own— three pretty pups, who looked just like their mother, and one mischievous Scamp, who clearly took after his father.

WALT DISNEY'S
Peter Pan

In a quiet street in London lived the Darling
family. There were Father and Mother Darling,
Wendy, Michael, and John, as well as the children's
nursemaid, Nana—a Saint Bernard.

At bedtime in the nursery, Wendy always told
wonderful stories about Peter Pan and Never Land, a
magical place with mermaids and fairies—and wicked
pirates, too.

John and Michael liked best of all to play pirate.
They had some fine slashing duels between Peter Pan
and his archenemy, the pirate Captain Hook.

Father Darling did not like this kind of play. He
blamed it on Wendy's childish stories of Peter Pan.

"It is time for Wendy to grow up," decided Father Darling. "This is your last night in the nursery, Wendy girl."

All the children were much upset at that. Without Wendy, there would be no more stories of Peter Pan!

That very evening, who should come to the nursery but Peter Pan, and a fairy named Tinker Bell! It seemed Peter had been out looking for his lost shadow. When he overheard that Wendy was to be moved from the nursery, he hit upon a plan.

"I'll take you to Never Land with me, to tell stories to my Lost Boys!" he decided as Wendy sewed his shadow back on.

Wendy thought that was a lovely idea—if Michael
and John could go, too. So Peter Pan taught them all
to fly—with happy thoughts and faith and trust, and
a sprinkling of Tinker Bell's pixie dust. Then out the
nursery window they sailed, heading for Never Land,
while Nana barked frantically below.

Back in Never Land, Captain Hook was
grumbling about Peter Pan. You see, once, in a
fair fight long ago, Peter Pan had cut off one of the
pirate captain's hands, so that he had to wear a hook
instead. Then Pan threw the hand to a crocodile, who
enjoyed the taste of Hook so much that he had been
lurking around ever since, hoping to nibble at the rest
of him. Fortunately for the pirate, the crocodile had
also swallowed a clock. He went "ticktock" when he
came near, which gave a warning to Captain Hook.

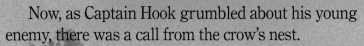

Now, as Captain Hook grumbled about his young enemy, there was a call from the crow's nest.

"Peter Pan ahoy!"

"What? Where?" shouted Hook, twirling his spyglass around in the sky. And then he spied Peter and the children pausing for a rest on a cloud. "Swoggle me eyes, it *is* Pan!" Hook gloated. "Pipe up the crew. . . . Man the guns. . . . We'll get him this time at last!"

"Oh, Peter, it's just as I dreamed it would be—
mermaid lagoon and all," Wendy said as a cannonball
ripped through the cloud beneath their feet.

"Look out!" cried Pan. "Tinker Bell, take Wendy
and the boys to the island. I'll stay here and draw
Hook's fire!"

Away flew Tinker Bell, as fast as she could go. In
her naughty little heart, she hoped the children would
fall behind and be lost. She was especially jealous of the
Wendy girl, who seemed to have won Peter Pan's heart.

Straight through the Never Land jungle Tink flew,
down into a clearing beside Hangman's Tree. She
landed on a toadstool, bounced to a shiny leaf, and *pop!*
a secret door opened for her in the knot of the old
hollow tree.

Zip! Down a slippery tunnel Tink slid. She landed
at the bottom in an underground room—the secret
house of Peter Pan.

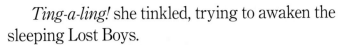

Ting-a-ling! she tinkled, trying to awaken the sleeping Lost Boys.

At last, rather grumpily, they woke up and stretched as they listened to Tinker Bell.

"What? Pan wants us to shoot down a terrible Wendy bird? Lead us to it!" they shouted, and out they hurried.

When Wendy and Michael and John appeared,
flying wearily, the Lost Boys tried to pelt them with
stones and sticks—especially the "Wendy bird." Down
tumbled Wendy, all of her happy thoughts destroyed—
without them no one can fly.

"Hurray! We got the Wendy bird!" the Lost Boys
shouted.

But then Peter Pan arrived. How angry he was
when he discovered that the boys had tried to shoot
down Wendy, even though he had caught her before
she could be hurt.

"I brought her to be a mother to us all and to
tell us stories," he said.

"Come on, Wendy," said Peter. "I'll show you the mermaids. Boys, take Michael and John to hunt some Indians."

So Peter and Wendy flew away, and the boys marched off through the forest, planning to capture some Indians. There were wild animals all around, but the boys never thought to be afraid, and not a creature harmed them as they went through the thick woods.

"First we'll surround the Indians," John decided. "Then we'll take them by surprise."

John's plan worked splendidly, but it was the Indians who used it. Disguised as moving trees, they quietly surrounded the boys and took *them* by surprise!

Soon, bound with ropes, the row of boys marched
away, led by the Indians to their village on the cliff.

"Don't worry, the Indians are our friends," the
Lost Boys said, but the chief looked stern.

Meanwhile, on the other side of the island, Wendy
and Peter were visiting the mermaids in their peaceful
mermaid lagoon. As they were chatting together,
Peter suddenly said, "Hush!"

A boat from the pirate ship was going by. In it
were wicked Captain Hook and Smee, the pirate cook.
And at the stern, all bound with ropes, sat Princess
Tiger Lily, daughter of the Indian chief.

"We'll make her talk," sneered Captain Hook.

"She'll tell us where Peter Pan lives, or we'll
leave her tied to slippery Skull Rock, where the tide
will wash over her."

But proud and loyal Tiger Lily would not say a
single word.

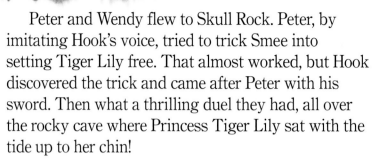

Peter and Wendy flew to Skull Rock. Peter, by imitating Hook's voice, tried to trick Smee into setting Tiger Lily free. That almost worked, but Hook discovered the trick and came after Peter with his sword. Then what a thrilling duel they had, all over the rocky cave where Princess Tiger Lily sat with the tide up to her chin!

Peter won the duel and rescued Tiger Lily just in the nick of time. Then away he flew to the Indian village, to see the princess safely home. And Wendy went along behind.

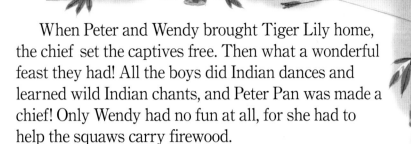

When Peter and Wendy brought Tiger Lily home, the chief set the captives free. Then what a wonderful feast they had! All the boys did Indian dances and learned wild Indian chants, and Peter Pan was made a chief! Only Wendy had no fun at all, for she had to help the squaws carry firewood.

"I've had enough of Never Land," she thought grumpily. "I'm ready to go home right now!"

 While the Indian celebration was at its height, Smee the pirate cook captured Tinker Bell and took her back to the pirate ship. He presented Tink to Captain Hook.

 "Ah, Miss Bell," said Hook sympathetically, "I've heard how badly Peter Pan has treated you since that scheming girl Wendy came. How nice it would be if we could kidnap her and take her off to sea to scrub the decks and cook for the pirate crew!"

 Tink tinkled happily at the thought.

"But, alas," sighed Hook, "we don't know where Pan's house is, so we cannot get rid of Wendy for you."

Tink thought this over. "You won't hurt Peter?" she asked, in solemn tinkling tones.

"Of course not!" promised Hook.

Then she marched to a map of Never Land and traced a path to Peter's hidden house.

"Thank you, my dear," said wicked Captain Hook, and he locked her up in a lantern cage and went off to capture Peter Pan!

That night, when Wendy tucked the children into their beds in the underground house, she talked to them about home and Mother. Soon they were all so homesick that they wanted to leave at once for home. Wendy invited all the Lost Boys to come and live with the Darling family. Only Peter refused to go. He simply looked the other way as Wendy and the boys told him good-bye and climbed the tunnel to Hangman's Tree.

Up in the woods near Hangman's Tree waited
Hook and his pirate band. As each boy came out, a
hand was clapped over his mouth and he was quickly
tied up with ropes. Last of all came Wendy. *Zip, zip,*
she was bound up, too, and the crew marched off with
their load of children, back to their pirate ship.

"Blast it!" muttered Hook. "We still don't have Pan!"

So he and Smee left a wicked bomb, wrapped as
a gift from Wendy, for poor Peter to find. Very soon,
they hoped, Peter would open it and blow himself
straight out of Never Land.

On the pirate ship, Captain Hook demanded that
Wendy and the boys become pirates.

"Never!" Wendy cried.

"Then you shall be the first to walk the plank,
my dear," said Hook.

In the excitement, no one noticed that Tinker
Bell escaped and flew off.

Wendy said good-bye, bravely walked out the long
narrow plank, and disappeared.

Everyone listened, waiting for a splash, but none
came! Then they heard a familiar sound. It was Pan!
Warned by Tinker Bell, he had arrived just in time to
scoop up Wendy in midair and fly her to safety.

"This time you have gone too far, Hook," Peter cried.

He swooped down from the rigging, all set for a duel. And what a duel it was!

While they fought, Tinker Bell slashed the ropes that bound the boys, and they beat the pirates into jumping overboard and rowing away in their boat. Then Peter knocked Hook's sword overboard, and Hook jumped, too. When the children last saw the wicked Captain Hook, he was swimming for the boat, with the crocodile *ticktock*ing hungrily behind him.

Peter Pan took command of the pirate ship. "Heave those halyards. Up with the jib. We're sailing to London," he cried.

"Oh, Michael! John!" cried Wendy. "We're going home!"

And sure enough, with happy thoughts and faith and trust, and a liberal sprinkling of pixie dust, away flew that pirate ship through the skies till the gangplank was run out to the Darlings' nursery windowsill. But now that they had arrived, the Lost Boys did not want to stay. "We've sort of decided to stick with Pan," they said.

So Wendy, John, and Michael waved good-bye as
Peter Pan's ship sailed off through the sky, taking the
Lost Boys home to Never Land, where they still live today.

From the smallest ant to the largest elephant,
every living thing has a place in the great Circle of Life.
Mufasa's place was as king of the lions. Sarabi was the
queen. And their newborn cub, Simba, would one day
take his father's place as the Lion King.

But on this day, little Simba rested in the hands of the
wise baboon Rafiki, who sprinkled the cub with dust
and welcomed the future king to the great Circle of Life.

Mufasa's brother, Scar, did not attend the ceremony.
He was not happy that Simba was next in line to rule
the Pride Lands. For Scar had always wanted to be king.

Time passed, and Simba grew. Early one morning, Mufasa took him to the top of Pride Rock. "Simba, look," he said. "Everything the light touches is our kingdom."

"Wow!" the young lion said. Then he asked, "What about the shadowy place?"

"That's beyond our borders. You must never go there, Simba!" warned Mufasa.

Later Simba proudly told his uncle, Scar, "Someday I'm gonna rule the whole kingdom! Well . . . everything except the shadowy place. My father said I can't go there."

"He's absolutely right," Scar slyly agreed. "An elephant graveyard is no place for a young prince. Only the bravest lions go there."

Scar knew Simba would want to prove that he was brave. He said nothing as Simba ran off to ask his friend Nala to explore the mysterious Shadow Lands with him.

When the friends arrived at the Shadow Lands, they discovered an eerie, steamy place filled with elephant bones.

"It's so creepy," whispered Nala nervously.

"C'mon!" said Simba. "Let's check it out."

Zazu, the king's minister, had been looking for the cubs. When he caught up with them, he warned, "We are too far from the Pride Lands. It is dangerous!"

"Hee-hee-hee-hee-hee!" Strange laughter rang out. It belonged to three hyenas—Banzai, Shenzi, and Ed—who slinked out from an elephant skull.

When Zazu told the hyenas he was Mufasa's minister, they realized that Simba was the future king.

"He's a king fit for a meal," Banzai snickered. The hyenas chased Simba and Nala.

Suddenly a thunderous ROARRRR! rattled rocks and bones. It was the roar of Mufasa, the Lion King! The frightened hyenas ran away.

That evening Mufasa had a talk with Simba. "Being brave doesn't mean you go looking for trouble," he told his son.

"Dad," Simba asked suddenly, "we'll always be together, right?"

Mufasa gazed up at the sparkling heavens. "The great kings of the past look down on us from those stars," he said. "Whenever you feel alone, remember that those kings will always be there to guide you. And so will I."

Although Scar was angry with the hyenas for letting Simba go, he made a bargain with them. If they helped make him king, they could have the run of the Pride Lands.

So Scar brought Simba to a vast gorge and promised the cub a wonderful surprise if he would just wait on a certain rock. Scar then signaled to the hyenas.

The surprise turned out to be a stampeding herd of wildebeests, with the hyenas urging the herd on. The earth trembled. The wildebeests ran into the gorge, heading straight for Simba. He sought safety in a tree, but the branch bent under his weight.

Just before Simba would have fallen beneath the pounding hooves, Mufasa grabbed him and carried him to a rocky ledge. Then, through the thick, swirling dust, Simba saw his father disappear under the thundering herd.

When the stampede had passed, Simba found his
father lying lifeless at the foot of a cliff. What Simba
did not know was that Scar had pushed his brother off
the rock!

"If it weren't for you, the king would still be alive,"
lied Scar, appearing at Simba's side.

"He tried to save me," said the cub, sobbing. "It was
an accident."

"Run away, Simba," Scar advised. "Run away and
never return."

Scar watched as Simba ran away. Then he sent his hyenas to kill the cub.

But when the hyenas reached a thorny thicket, they stopped. "He'll never survive in the desert," they reasoned. And so they returned to Pride Rock—and their new king, Scar.

Under the burning desert sun, Simba surely would
have died if it had not been for two curious creatures—
Timon the meerkat and Pumbaa the warthog.

Timon and Pumbaa felt sorry for the cub. They took him to their jungle home and taught him how to live by Timon's philosophy, *hakuna matata,* which meant "no worries." They also taught the cub to eat insects.

Simba tried to put the past behind him. But one clear night, the stars reminded him of the old kings and his father, Mufasa.

Then one day a lioness chased Pumbaa. Simba rushed to protect his friend.

"Nala!" he cried.

"Simba?" the lioness said. "I thought you were dead." The friends embraced. Then Nala told Simba that under cruel King Scar, the Pride Lands had become barren and the animals were starving. Hyenas were everywhere.

But Simba refused to go back and take his place as the Lion King. He did not feel worthy.

That night, wise old Rafiki found Simba alone. He
led Simba to a small pool.

Simba saw his father's face in the water. Then he
heard his father's voice. "Simba, look inside yourself,"
Mufasa said. "You are my son and the one true king.
You must take your place in the Circle of Life."

So Simba set out for the Pride Lands to confront the false king. Later his friends Nala, Timon, and Pumbaa joined him.

"I'm surprised to see you alive," sneered Scar as Simba approached Pride Rock.

"I've come back to take my place as king," declared Simba.

With an angry snarl, Scar forced Simba to the edge of a cliff. As Simba struggled to hold on, Scar leaned down and whispered, "Here's my little secret, Simba. You didn't kill your father. I did."

Simba's heart filled with rage, and the strength of ten lions surged through him. He struggled up onto the rock, leaped on Scar, and the battle began!

Nala bravely led the other lionesses against the hyenas. Even Timon and Pumbaa joined the fight. The battle raged until all the hyenas ran from Pride Rock.

Simba chased Scar to the top of Pride Rock and cornered him.

Scar whimpered, "No. Please. Have pity on me."

"Run away, Scar," said Simba. "Run away and never return."

But when Simba turned his back, Scar attacked! Quick as the lightning that flashed above, Simba sent Scar flying over the cliff to the hungry hyenas below.

So Scar's evil reign ended, and Simba took his rightful place as the Lion King. In time, King Simba and Queen Nala had a cub of their own.

Way atop Pride Rock, their child rested in the hands of the wise baboon Rafiki, who sprinkled the cub with dust and welcomed her to the great Circle of Life.

Many strange legends are told of the jungles of far-off India. They speak of Bagheera the black panther, and of Baloo the bear. They tell of Kaa the sly python, and of the lord of the jungle, the great tiger Shere Khan. But of all these legends, none is so strange as the story of a small boy named Mowgli.

A child, left all alone in the jungle, was found by Bagheera the panther. Bagheera could not give the small, helpless Man-cub care and nourishment, so he took the boy to the den of a wolf family with young cubs of their own.

That is how it happened that Mowgli, as the Man-cub came to be called, was raised among the wolves.

Mowgli had lived with the wolves for ten years when the wolf pack called a meeting at Council Rock. "As you know," said Akela, the leader of the pack, "Shere Khan the tiger has returned. If he learns that our pack is harboring a Man-cub, danger will be doubled for all our families. The Man-cub can no longer stay with the pack."

Out of the shadows stepped Bagheera the panther. "Perhaps I can be of help," said Bagheera. "I know of a Man-village where he'll be safe."

So it was arranged, and when the
greenish light of the jungle morning
slipped through the leaves, Bagheera
and Mowgli set out.

All day they walked, and when
night fell, they slept on a high branch
of a giant banyan tree. All this seemed
like an adventure to Mowgli. But when
he learned that he was to leave the
jungle, he was horrified.

"No!" cried Mowgli. "I want to stay in the jungle. I'm not afraid. I can look out for myself."

He slipped down a length of trailing vine and ran away.

Mowgli soon met a bumbling bear named Baloo.
Baloo played games with Mowgli and taught him
to live a life of ease. There were coconuts to crack,
bananas to peel, and sweet, juicy pawpaws to pick
from jungle trees.

Colonel Hathi, the proud old leader
of the elephant herd, tried to train young
Mowgli in military drills as he led his
troop, trumpeting down the jungle trails.
Mowgli was having such fun in
the jungle!

But the jungle *was* dangerous.

Sly old Kaa the python would have loved to squeeze Mowgli tight in his coils.

But Shere Khan the tiger was the real danger to Mowgli. That was because Shere Khan, like all tigers, had a hatred of man.

There were other dangers, too.

One day, Baloo and Mowgli were enjoying a dip in a jungle river. Suddenly, down swooped the monkey folk. They snatched Mowgli from the water before Baloo knew what was happening.

They tossed him through the air from hand to hand and swung away with him through the trees.

Off in the jungle, Bagheera heard Mowgli's cry and came with a leap and a bound.

"The monkeys have carried him off!" gasped Baloo.

Bagheera and Baloo raced to the ruined city where the monkeys made their home. They found Mowgli a prisoner of the monkey king.

"Teach me the secret of man's red fire," the monkey king ordered Mowgli, "so I can be like you."

It took quite a fight for Bagheera and Baloo to rescue Mowgli!

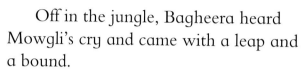

"Look, Mowgli," said Baloo. "I gotta take you to the Man-village."

But alas, the boy would not listen. He kicked up his heels and ran away again.

This time, his wanderings led him to the high grass, where Shere Khan lay waiting, smiling a hungry smile.

When Mowgli caught sight of the tiger, Shere Khan asked, "Well, Man-cub, aren't you going to run?"

But Mowgli did not have the wisdom to be afraid. "Why should I run?" he asked, staring at Shere Khan as the tiger gathered himself to pounce. "You don't scare me."

"That foolish boy!" growled Bagheera,
who had crept close just in time to hear Mowgli.
   Both Bagheera and Baloo flung themselves
upon the lord of the jungle, to save Mowgli
once more.

They were brave and strong, but the tiger was mighty of tooth and claw.

There was a flash of lightning, and a dead tree nearby caught fire. Mowgli snatched a burning branch and tied it to Shere Khan's tail. The tiger, terrified, ran away. Mowgli was very pleased with himself as he strutted between the two weary warriors, Bagheera and Baloo.

A little later, Mowgli reached the Man-village. From ahead came a sound he did not know. He peeked through a bush. It was the song of a village girl who had come to fill her water jug.

As he listened to the soft notes of her song, Mowgli felt that he must follow the girl. He crept up the path to the village, drawn by the girl and her song.

Baloo and Bagheera watched the boy's small figure as long as it could be seen. When Mowgli vanished inside the village gate, Bagheera sighed a deep sigh.

"It was bound to happen," he said. "Mowgli is where he belongs now."

One night, the Evening Star shone down on a tiny village. Only one house still had a light burning, and that was the workshop of Geppetto, the kindly old woodcarver. He was busy carving a little puppet.

"Isn't Pinocchio almost like a real boy?" he chuckled.

Climbing into bed, the old man mumbled,
"I wish you *were* a real boy, Pinocchio."

Jiminy Cricket overheard Geppetto's wish. He
had seen how kind and gentle the woodcarver
was, and he felt sorry because the lonely old
man's wish could never come true.

Suddenly a shimmering light filled the room.
Then a beautiful lady dressed in shining blue
appeared. She raised her wand and said:

"Wake, Pinocchio! Skip and run! Good Geppetto needs a son!" Pinocchio blinked his eyes and raised his wooden arms.

"I can move!" he cried. "I'm a real boy!"

"No," the Blue Fairy said sadly. "You have life, but to become a real boy, you must prove yourself brave, truthful, and unselfish."

And Jiminy Cricket would help.

The next morning, Geppetto couldn't believe his eyes. There was his puppet, laughing and talking and running!

"It's true, Father!" Pinocchio cried. "I'm alive!"

After the initial joy was over, Geppetto said, "But now, Pinocchio, you must go to school. Study hard! Then you'll soon become a real boy!"

Meanwhile, Jiminy Cricket had overslept and now jumped up in a great hurry. He caught up with Pinocchio just as the silly little puppet was walking off with the worst pair of scoundrels in the whole countryside—J. Worthington Foulfellow and Gideon.

The villains convinced Pinocchio that he should forget about school and become an actor.

"But, Pinoke!" cried Jiminy. "What will your father say?"

Pinocchio said, "Father will be proud of me!"

Soon they came to a marionette theater. When its owner, Stromboli, saw Pinocchio, his small, evil eyes glistened. "What a drawing card!" he exclaimed. "A puppet without strings!"

The fox nodded. "And he's yours," he said, smiling greedily and holding out his paw, "for a certain price, of course!"

That night Pinocchio sang and danced. The audience cheered for more. A puppet without strings! It was a miracle!

But when Pinocchio started to head home for the night, Stromboli snarled at him. "You're mine, and you stay here!" And *bang!* Before Pinocchio could resist, he was locked in a birdcage!

"Oh, Jiminy," Pinocchio sobbed, "why didn't I go to school? I'll never see my father again!"

Suddenly the Blue Fairy appeared before the sad friends.

"I'll help you this time," she said, "because you are truly sorry. Run home now, Pinocchio, and be a good son, or you'll never become a real boy!"

"Whew!" Pinocchio sighed thankfully. "Let's go home!"

He and Jiminy started running as fast as they could, but whom should they bump into but Foulfellow and Gideon!

This time Foulfellow persuaded the gullible puppet to forget his good resolutions and take a "rest cure" on Pleasure Island.

"You promised to go right home!" Jiminy cried.

"But Foulfellow says I need a rest after my terrible experience."

They came to a coach bound for Pleasure Island. It was pulled by small donkeys and filled with noisy boys. As Pinocchio climbed aboard, Jiminy saw the evil-looking coachman slip Foulfellow a heavy bag. Again the fox had sold Pinocchio!

After boarding a ferry, the coach docked at Pleasure Island. Here streets were paved with cookies, and fountains spouted lemonade.

Pinocchio soon made friends with a young bully called Lampwick who was always in the middle of mischief.

Jiminy was not happy. He shouted at the puppet to go home.

"Don't tell me you're scared of a beetle!" Lampwick snickered.

Jiminy was about to march off when all of a sudden Lampwick and Pinocchio groaned.

The boys were sprouting donkey ears!

"It's donkey fever," whispered Jiminy, horrified. "You were lazy, good-for-nothing boys, so you're turning into donkeys!"

They quickly dashed through the streets.

As they rounded a corner, they saw the coachman herding a bunch of braying donkeys, many of which still wore boys' hats and shoes.

TO THE SALT MINES

Pinocchio and Jiminy managed to climb up the wall surrounding the island, but Lampwick had already turned into a donkey.

There was nothing they could do. With a lump in his throat, Pinocchio followed Jiminy and dove into the sea to escape.

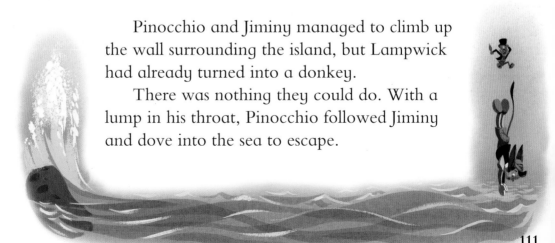

They had a long, hard journey home. By the time they came to the village, it was winter. They hurried to Geppetto's door and pounded on it. But the house was empty!

Just then a gust of wind blew a piece of paper around the corner. "Hey, Pinoke!" Jiminy exclaimed. "It's a letter!"

Dear Pinocchio,

I heard you had gone to Pleasure Island, so Figaro,
Cleo, and I started off in a small boat to find you. Just
as we came in sight of the island, out of the sea rose
Monstro, the giant whale. He opened his jaws; in we
went. Now, dear son, we are living in the belly
of the whale. But there is very little to eat here,
and we cannot exist much longer, so I fear you
will never again see

Your loving father,
Geppetto

For a while, they were both silent, too sad to speak. Then Pinocchio stood tall and said, "I am going to save my father!"

Just then a dove wearing a golden crown appeared. "I will take you," she said. "Climb on." Then she spread her wings and flew and flew until they reached the seashore.

Pinocchio and Jiminy did not know that the dove was the Blue Fairy in disguise, and that it was she who had brought them Geppetto's letter.

When the dove was out of sight, Pinocchio tied a big stone to his donkey tail. Then he and Jiminy leaped off the cliff into the ocean below.

As soon as they reached the sandy bottom, Pinocchio scrambled to his feet. "Come on," he said. "Let's find Monstro."

"We'll never find him," muttered Jiminy. "We're probably looking in the wrong ocean!"

Jiminy was wrong. Very near them floated the whale they were looking for, fast asleep. Inside the whale was Geppetto. He had set up a crude home from the ships the whale had swallowed, and every day he fished in the whale's belly. But now that Monstro was sleeping, no fish came in.

"Not a bite for days, Figaro," Geppetto said mournfully to his cat. "If Monstro doesn't wake soon, we'll all starve."

Just then Geppetto felt a nibble. "Food, Figaro!" he cried. But when the catch was landed, it was only a cookbook called *How to Cook Fish*.

It was a solemn moment. All felt that the end was near.

And then the whale moved!

Monstro gave an upward lunge, and through his jaws rushed a wall of water. With it came fish—a whole school of tuna!

Pinocchio saw Monstro coming at him. He held on to a fish and was eaten, too.

Soon Geppetto was pulling fish after fish out of the water. He was so busy, he almost didn't notice Pinocchio getting pulled on board.

"Oh, my own dear son!" he exclaimed. "Is it really you?"

They were thrilled to see each other again. Now if they could only get out of the whale! Pinocchio had a plan.

The puppet set fire to a pile of crates. As the
fire began to smoke, they jumped onto a raft.
Soon the whale gave a monstrous SNEEZE!

Out went the raft, past those crunching jaws,
into the open sea!

But they were not yet free. The angry whale
plunged after them and splintered their frail craft.

Geppetto was sinking. "My son, save
yourself!" he cried.

But the brave puppet kept him afloat as giant
waves swept them toward the shore.

Geppetto lay on the beach, gratitude filling his
heart. And then he saw Pinocchio lying beside him,
still, cold, and pale! The old man was heartbroken.

Geppetto gathered poor Pinocchio into his arms and headed home. Then he prayed.

Suddenly a ray of starlight appeared. A soft voice said, ". . . And someday, when you have proven yourself brave, truthful, and unselfish, you will be a real boy. . . ."

Pinocchio sat up. He looked at himself and felt his arms and legs. Then he knew!

"Father! Look at me!" he cried joyfully.

The Blue Fairy's promise had come true! Pinocchio was a real, live boy!

WALT DISNEY'S
Bambi

Bambi came into the world in the middle of a thicket, one of those little hidden forest glades which seem to be open but are really screened in on all sides.

The magpie was the first to discover him.

"This is quite an occasion," he said. "It isn't often that a young prince is born. Congratulations!"

Bambi's mother looked up. "Thank you,"
she said quietly. Then she nudged her sleeping
baby gently with her nose. "Wake up," she whispered.
"Wake up!"

The fawn lifted his head and looked around. He
looked frightened and edged closer to his mother's body.
She licked him reassuringly and nudged him again. He
pushed up on his thin hind legs, trying to stand. His
forelegs kept crumpling, but at last they bore his weight
and he stood beside his mother.

"What are you going to name the young prince?"
asked the baby rabbit.

"I'll call him Bambi," the mother answered.

"Bambi," repeated the rabbit. "That's a good name. My name's Thumper." And he hopped away with his mother and sisters.

The little fawn sank down and nestled close to his mother. She licked his spotted red coat softly.

The birds and animals slipped away through the forest, leaving the thicket in peace and quiet.

The forest was beautiful in the summer. The trees
stood still under the blue sky, and out of the earth
came troops of flowers, unfolding their red, white, and
yellow stars.

Bambi liked to follow his mother down the forest
paths, so narrow that the thick leafy bushes stroked
his flanks as he passed. Sometimes a branch tripped
him or a bush tangled about his legs, but always his
mother walked easily and surely.

There were friends all along these forest paths. The opossums, hanging by their long tails from the branches of a tree, said, "Hello, Prince Bambi."

As Bambi and his mother reached a little clearing in the forest, they met Thumper and his family.

"Come on, Bambi," said Thumper, "let's play."
And Bambi began to run on his stiff, spindly
legs. Then he saw a family of birds on a low branch.
He stared at them.

"These are birds, Bambi," Thumper said.

"Birds," said Bambi slowly. It was his first word. When he saw a butterfly flutter across the path, he cried, "Bird, bird!" again.

"No, Bambi," said Thumper. "That's not a bird. It's a butterfly."

Then Bambi saw a clump of yellow flowers, and he bounded toward them.

"Butterfly!" he cried.

"No, Bambi," said Thumper. "Flower."

Suddenly he drew back. Out from the bed of flowers came a small black head with two gleaming eyes.

"Flower!" said Bambi.

"That's not a flower," Thumper giggled. "Skunk."

"Flower," said Bambi again.

"The young prince can call me Flower if he wants to," said the skunk. "I don't mind. In fact, I like it."

Bambi had made another friend.

One morning Bambi and his mother walked down a
path where the fawn had never been. A few steps more
and they would be in a meadow.

"Wait here until I call you," she said. "The meadow is
not always safe."

She listened in all directions and called, "Come."

Bambi bounded out. Joy seized him and he leaped
into the air, three, four, five times.

"Catch me!" his mother cried, and she bounded ahead.

Bambi started after her. He felt as if he were flying,
without any effort.

As he stopped for breath, he saw standing beside him
a small fawn.

"Hello," she said, moving nearer to him.

Bambi, shy, bounded away to where he saw his friend, Flower the skunk, playing. He pretended he did not see the new little fawn.

"Don't be afraid, Bambi," his mother said.

"That is little Faline; her mother is your Aunt Ena."

Soon Bambi and Faline were racing around hillocks.

Suddenly there was a sound of hoofbeats, and figures came bursting out of the woods. They were the stags.

One of the stags was larger and stronger than all the others. This was the great Prince of the Forest, very brave and wise.

The great stag uttered one dreadful word: "MAN!"

Instantly birds and animals rushed toward the woods. As Bambi and his mother disappeared into the trees, they heard behind them on the meadow loud, roaring noises, terrifying to Bambi's ears.

Later, as Bambi and his mother lay safely in their thicket, his mother explained. "MAN. Bambi—it was MAN in the meadow. He brings danger and death to the forest with his long stick that roars and spurts flames. Someday you will understand."

One morning Bambi woke up shivering with cold. His nose told him there was something strange in the world. When he looked out through the thicket he saw everything covered with white.

"It's snow, Bambi," his mother said. "Go ahead and walk out."

Cautiously Bambi stepped on the surface of the snow and saw his feet sink down in it. The air was calm and the sun on the white snow sparkled. Bambi was delighted.

As he walked, stepping high and carefully, a breeze shifted a branch above him ever so slightly, just enough to tip a heavy load of snow on Bambi's head. He jumped high in the air, startled and frightened, then ran on, licking the snow from his nose. It tasted good—clean and cool.

Thumper was playing on the ice-covered pond, and Bambi trotted gingerly down the slope and out onto the smooth ice, too. His front legs shot forward, his rear legs slipped back and down he crashed! He looked up to see Thumper laughing at him.

He finally lurched to his feet and skidded across the ice dizzily, landing headfirst in a snowbank on the shore.

As he pulled himself out of the drift, he and Thumper heard a faint sound of snoring. Peering down into a deep burrow, they saw the little skunk lying peacefully asleep on a bed of withered flowers.

"Wake up, Flower!" Bambi called.

"Is it spring yet?" Flower asked sleepily.

"No, winter's just beginning," said Bambi.

"I'm hibernating," the little skunk smiled. "Flowers always sleep in the winter." And he dozed off again.

So Bambi learned about winter. It was a difficult time for all the animals in the forest. Food grew scarce. Sometimes Bambi and his mother had to strip bark from trees and eat it.

At last, when it seemed they could find no more to eat, there was a change in the air. Thin sunshine filtered through the bare branches, and the air was a little warmer. That day, too, Bambi's mother dug under the soft snow and found a few blades of pale green grass.

Bambi and his mother were nibbling at the grass when they suddenly smelled MAN. As they lifted their heads, there came a deafening roar like thunder.

"Quick, Bambi," his mother said, "run for the thicket. Don't stop, no matter what happens."

Bambi darted away and heard his mother's footsteps behind him. Then came another roar from MAN's guns. Bambi dashed among the trees in terrified speed. But when he came at last to the thicket his mother was not in sight. He sniffed the air for her smell, listened for her hoofbeats. There was nothing!

Bambi raced out into the forest, calling wildly for his mother. Silently the old stag appeared beside him.

"Your mother can't be with you any more," the stag said. "You must learn to walk alone."

In silence Bambi followed the great stag off through the snow filled forest.

Soon it was spring. Everything was turning green, and the leaves looked fresh and smiling.

Suddenly Bambi looked up and saw another deer.

"Hello, Bambi," said the other deer. "Don't you remember me? I'm Faline." Bambi stared at her. Faline was now a graceful and beautiful doe.

A strange excitement swept over Bambi. When Faline trotted up and licked his face, Bambi started to dash away. But after a few steps he stopped. Faline dashed into the bushes and Bambi followed.

Suddenly Ronno, a buck with big antlers, stood between Bambi and Faline.

"Stop!" he cried. "Faline is going with me."

Bambi stood still as Ronno nudged Faline down the path. Suddenly he shot forward, and they charged together with a crash.

Again and again they came together, forehead to forehead. Then a prong broke from Ronno's antlers, a terrific blow tore open his shoulder, and he fell to the ground, sliding down a rocky embankment.

As Ronno limped off into the forest, Bambi and Faline walked away through the woods. At night they trotted onto the meadow, where they stood in the moonlight, listening to the east wind and the west wind calling to each other.

Early one morning in the autumn Bambi sniffed the scent of MAN.

The great stag came and said, "Yes, Bambi, it's MAN, with tents and campfires. We must go to the hills."

Bambi ran back to the thicket for Faline. The sounds of MAN and the barking of dogs came closer.

He lunged at the dogs and called, "Run, Faline!"

The roar of a gun crashed almost beside him, but he dashed ahead as a killing pain shot through him.

The old stag appeared and said, "The forest has caught fire from the flames of MAN's campfires. We must go to the river." They plunged into the raging fire, and then fell into cool, rushing water.

Panting and breathless, they struggled onto a safe shore, already crowded with other animals.

With a cry of joy Faline came running to him and gently licked the wound on his shoulder.

Together they stood on the shore, and watched the flames destroy their forest home.

But soon spring came again, and green leaves and grass and flowers covered the scars left by the fire.

Again news went through the forest. "Come along, come to the thicket."

At the thicket, the squirrels and rabbits and birds were peering through the undergrowth at Faline and two spotted fawns.

And not far away was Bambi, the proud father, and the new great Prince of the Forest.

Walt Disney's
DUMBO

I t was spring . . . spring in the circus!

After the long winter's rest, it was time to set out again on the open road.

"Toot! Toot!" whistled Casey Jones, the locomotive of the circus train.

"All aboard!" shouted the ringmaster.

The acrobats, the jugglers, the tumblers, the snake charmers scrambled to their places on the train. The keepers locked the animal cages. Then with a jiggety jerk and a brisk puff-puff, off sped Casey Jones! The circus was on its way!

Everyone was singing. Everyone was happy.

Happiest of all was Mrs. Jumbo, for in her stall was a chubby, brand-new baby elephant. Though the other animals called the baby Dumbo, his mother loved him dearly. Even though his ears *were* big.

All night, while the baby animals slept, Casey Jones whistled and puffed, hauling the long train to the city where the circus was to open its show.

It was dark when he pulled into the station. Rain
poured down hard, but the circus began to unload. The
roustabouts jumped down from the freight cars.

They lighted torches and stuck them in the ground.
Men and animals came bustling out of the train into
the windy, wet night. Mrs. Jumbo worked with the
others, and her baby helped a little.

By morning the rain had stopped, the tent was all
set up, and the circus was busy getting ready for the big
parade. The band played. Everyone fell in line.

Then off pranced the gay procession down the main
street. There were creamy-white horses, licorice-
colored seals! There were lady acrobats in pink silk
tights, lions pacing in their gilded wagon-cages,
elephants marching with slow, even steps.

The crowds on the sidewalk cheered. Then,
suddenly, their eyes opened wide. They craned their
necks. "Look . . . look!" they cried. "Look at that silly
animal with the draggy ears! He *can't* be an
elephant . . . he must be a clown!"

Sadly, Dumbo toddled behind his mother, with his trunk clasped to her tail. He tried to hurry along faster so he wouldn't hear the laughter, but he stumbled. He tripped over his ears. Down he splashed into a puddle of mud. Now the crowds laughed even louder. Mrs. Jumbo scowled at them. She picked Dumbo up and carried him in her trunk the rest of the way.

When the parade finally came back to the tent, everyone hustled to get ready for the afternoon show. Mrs. Jumbo put Dumbo in her wooden bathtub, and as she scrubbed she whispered comforting words.

A gang of noisy boys came pushing in first for the afternoon show. "We want to see the elephant," they yelled, "–the one with the sailboat ears!"

"Look . . . there he is."

A boy grabbed one of Dumbo's ears and pulled it hard. Then he made an ugly face and stuck out his tongue.

Mrs. Jumbo couldn't stand it. She snatched the boy up with her trunk and spanked him, hard.

"Help!" he cried. "Help! Help!"

"What's going on here?" cried the ringmaster, rushing forward with his whip. "Tie her down!" he yelled.

Soon she was behind the bars in the prison wagon with a big sign that said: "Danger! Mad Elephant! Keep Out!"

The next day, they made Dumbo into a clown. They painted his face with a foolish grin and dressed him in a baby dress. On his head they put a bonnet. They used him in the most ridiculous act in the show– a make-believe fire. Every night he had to jump from the top of a blazing cardboard house, down into a firemen's net. The audience thought it a great joke. But Dumbo felt disgraced.

"He's a disgrace to us," the big animals agreed, and they turned their backs on him.

Hidden in a pile of hay was Timothy Mouse, the smallest animal with the circus.

"They can't treat the little fellow that way," he muttered. "Not while Timothy Mouse is around."

"Hey there, little fellow!" he called to Dumbo. "Don't be afraid. I'm your friend. I want to help you."

Timothy ran up toward Dumbo's ear. "We'll get your mother out of jail, you and I together, and we'll make you the star of the show. You'll be flying high!

"Say!" he went on, staring at Dumbo's ears. "Those ears are as good as wings. I'll teach you to fly!"

Quietly Dumbo crept out of the tent with Timothy, and soon they came to the prison car on a siding.

Dumbo told his mother all about the clown act, and how unhappy he was without her, and about the wonderful idea Timothy had for making him a success.

Mother Jumbo listened sympathetically, stroking
him gently with her trunk.

"Don't you worry, Baby," she told him. "You're
having a hard time now, and I'm sorry I can't be with
you to help. But just remember always to do your best
and, as Timothy says, you'll soon be flying high."

Then sadly they said good night, and Timothy and
Dumbo continued on their way. Out on the bare fields
in the starlight they went to work.

With Timothy as teacher Dumbo practiced running
and jumping and hopping.

He stretched out his wings and flapped them, 1-2-3-4. But hard as he tried, Dumbo could not leave the ground.

At last, almost too tired to stand, the two friends gave up and started gloomily back toward the sleeping circus.

"Don't worry, Dumbo," Timothy whispered as he curled up on Dumbo's hat brim for a good night's sleep. "We'll have you flying yet!"

So Dumbo fell asleep with a tired smile on his face and a beautiful dream in his heart. In the dream he was flying as easily and gracefully as a bird–soaring through the air, high above the circus. It was a wonderful dream, and it seemed very real to Dumbo.

When the morning sun arose, Timothy was the first to awaken. He blinked and looked up. Just above him, four old black crows sat and stared at him.

"Why . . . why . . . ," yawned Timothy, rubbing his eyes. "Where am I?"

"You're up in our tree," snapped the crows crossly. "That's where you are."

"*Tree?*" gasped Timothy. He looked around. Sure enough, there he was, sitting on a branch. He and Dumbo *were* up in a tree! The ground was far, far below. "But . . . but . . . how did we get here?" he stammered.

"*How!*" cackled the crows. "You and that elephant just came a-flyin' up!"

"Flying!" Timothy yelled. "Dumbo, Dumbo, wake up! Dumbo, we're up in a tree! You FLEW here!"

Slowly Dumbo opened his eyes. He glanced down. He gulped. Then he struggled to his feet. But suddenly he slipped on the smooth tree bark and fell. Down . . . down . . . down! He bounced from branch to branch, with Timothy clinging to his trunk. Plonk! They landed in a shallow pond just underneath the tree. The crows chuckled and cawed from above.

Timothy scrambled up out of the water and wrung out Dumbo's tail. "Dumbo," he panted. "You can fly! If you can fly when you're asleep, you can fly when you're awake. Your ears, Dumbo, they're your fortune!"

He grabbed one of Dumbo's wet ears and patted it. "You won't be a clown anymore. You'll be famous . . . the only flying elephant in the whole wide world!"

And Timothy and Dumbo began all over again to practice flying.

But it wasn't easy. Time after time, Dumbo tried to take off. Time after time, he sprawled out flat on his face. Soon the crows began to feel sorry for the little fellow. When Timothy told them all the sad things that had happened to Dumbo because of his big ears, they flew down and offered to help.

One of the crows took Timothy aside. "Flying's just like swimming," he whispered. "It's just a matter of believing that you can do it." He turned and snatched a long, black feather from his tail.

"Here, take this . . . tell the baby elephant it's a *magic* feather. Tell him if he holds it, he can fly." The boss crow winked and flew off.

Timothy handed Dumbo the feather and scurried up his trunk to the brim of his cap.

The trick worked like a charm. The very instant that Dumbo wrapped the tip of his trunk around the feather, flap . . . flap . . . flap! went his ears. Up into the air he soared like a bird! Over the tallest treetops he sailed. He glided, he dipped, he dived. Three times he circled over the heads of the cheering crows. Then he headed back to the circus grounds.

Timothy shouted, "We must keep your flying a secret—a surprise for your act in this afternoon's show."

No one noticed Dumbo when he and Timothy came quietly back. It was already time for Dumbo to get into his costume. Inside the walls of the cardboard house he had to wait all through the show until fire crackled up around him.

At last Timothy leaned down and handed him the feather. "In just a second, Dumbo," he whispered, "you'll be the most famous animal in all the world!"

Cr . . . rr . . . rr . . . ack! Cr . . . rr . . . rr . . . ack! crackled the fire. The clown act was on! Flames shot up around the cardboard house. Clang! Clang! roared the clown fire engine, rushing toward the blaze.

From the far end of the ring, a redheaded mother clown came running. "Save my baby!" she screamed. "He's on the top floor!"

The firemen brought a big net and held it out.

"Jump, my darling baby, jump!" shrieked the mother clown.

Dumbo jumped, but as he jumped the black feather slipped from his trunk and floated away. Now his magic was gone, and Dumbo plunged down like a stone.

"You can fly!" Timothy shouted frantically. "The feather's a fake. You can fly!"

Dumbo heard the shout and, doubtfully, spread his ears wide. Not two feet above the net he stopped his plunge and swooped up into the air!

A mighty gasp arose from the audience. They knew it couldn't be, but it was! *Dumbo was flying!*

While the crowd roared its delight, Dumbo did power dives, loops, spins, and barrel rolls. He swooped down to pick up peanuts and squirted a trunkful of water on the clowns.

The keepers freed Mrs. Jumbo and brought her to the tent in triumph to see her baby fly. So all of Dumbo's worries had come to an end.

By evening, Dumbo was a hero from coast to coast.

Timothy became Dumbo's manager, and he saw to it that Dumbo got a wonderful contract with a big salary and a pension for his mother.

167

The circus was renamed "Dumbo's Flying Circus," and Dumbo traveled in a special streamlined car. But best of all, he forgave everyone who had been unkind to him, for his heart was as big as his magical ears.

Pongo, Perdita, and their fifteen puppies lived in a cozy little house in London. Their humans lived there, too: Roger, who was tall and thin and played the piano, and Anita, who laughed a lot. They all got along splendidly and were very happy.

Then one day the doorbell rang, and in came Cruella De Vil, Anita's old friend from school.

"How marvelous!" Cruella said, stroking the puppies' soft fur.
"I'll take them all. The whole litter."

"I'm afraid we can't give them up," gasped Anita. "Poor Perdita . . .
she'd be heartbroken."

"Don't be ridiculous," said Cruella. "You can't possibly afford to
keep them."

"We are not selling the puppies," replied Roger, "and that's final!"
Furious, Cruella stamped out of the house.

One frosty night a few weeks later, Pongo and Perdita went out for a walk with Roger and Anita. The puppies were at home, asleep in their basket.

Suddenly, two men burst into the house. They put all the puppies into a big bag. Then they carried the bag out to their truck and sped away.

After being in the truck for what seemed like hours, the fifteen puppies found themselves in a room filled with many other Dalmatian puppies. On a couch in front of a television set were the two nasty men who had kidnapped them.

The other Dalmatians told them that the men worked for Cruella De Vil, who had bought the puppies from pet stores.

Back at home, Pongo and Perdita were horrified to find their puppies missing.

Pongo heard Roger tell Anita he suspected Cruella De Vil had stolen the puppies.

"Perdy, I'm afraid it's all up to us," said Pongo. "There's the Twilight Bark." The Twilight Bark was a system of long and short barks used by dogs to pass along news.

The next evening, Pongo and Perdita went on another walk with Roger and Anita. While the Dalmatians were out, they barked long and loud. They wanted all the dogs in London to be on the lookout for their puppies.

Pongo waited for someone to answer his barks. It was a very cold night, and most dogs were inside. Then Perdita added her bark to Pongo's, and at last they heard a reply.

It came from a Great Dane, who relayed the message to every other dog within barking range.

That night, the Twilight Bark even reached a quiet farm, where an old sheepdog known as the Colonel lay sleeping.

"Colonel, sir!" shouted Sergeant Tibs, a cat who lived on the farm. He had to let the Colonel know about the vital message coming in.

The Colonel lifted one shaggy ear to listen to the faint message. "It's from London. Fifteen spotted puddles stolen. Of course—puppies!" he cried.

"Two nights past, I heard puppy barking," Tibs said, remembering as he pointed to the De Vil mansion.

The Colonel barked a message back to London. Then he told Tibs, "I suppose we'd better investigate!"

They headed straight for the gloomy De Vil mansion. Tibs held on tight to the Colonel's back as he rushed through the snow.

Once they arrived, Tibs climbed onto the Colonel's shoulders. He peeked through an open window.

"Psst! Are you one of the fifteen stolen puppies?" he asked a little puppy without a collar.

"They're over there," said the puppy.

The men heard the noise and went to investigate. Tibs and the Colonel ran away, but not before promising to get help.

The next morning, Cruella De Vil arrived.

"It's got to be done tonight!" she cried.

"You couldn't get a half dozen coats out of the whole caboodle," complained one of her men, pointing to the puppies.

"Then we'll settle for half a dozen," said Cruella, "but do it!"

She dashed out and roared off in her car.

Sergeant Tibs and the Colonel had returned just in time to hear Cruella give the order. "Hey, kids, you'd better get out of here if you want to save your skins," Tibs whispered. Then he shoved one of the puppies toward a hole in the wall.

One by one, the other puppies followed.

Suddenly, the two thugs realized that the puppies were escaping. The chase was on! Tibs and the puppies scooted through the dark halls of the mansion. Soon they found themselves trapped at a dead end. The thugs raised their clubs to strike.

At that moment, Pongo and Perdita crashed through the window with a blast of glass and freezing air. The angry Dalmatian parents fought off the surprised men as all the puppies scampered to safety.

Once the dogs were safely outside, they thanked the Colonel and Tibs and said good-bye. Then they hurried toward London. Pongo and Perdita led the way, their fifteen puppies and all the other Dalmatian pups right behind them.

When they reached a frozen stream, they carefully crossed the slippery surface so they wouldn't leave paw prints. Then they resumed the race home.

All along their route, the Dalmatians were helped by other dogs. A black Labrador retriever arranged for them to ride to London in a moving van. The Dalmatians waited in a shed while the van was being fixed.

Suddenly, Cruella's big car pulled up outside. Somehow she had followed their tracks.

"Pongo," said Perdita. "How will we get to the van?"

Pongo noticed lots of ashes in the fireplace. If they all rolled in the soot, they would look just like black Labradors.

When the van was ready, the dogs marched outside. One after another, the soot-covered puppies were lifted into the van. Before Pongo had a chance to pick up the last one, a clump of snow fell from the shed onto the puppy.

Pongo snatched up the pup, but the snow had washed away the soot. From her car, Cruella could see the white fur and black spots.

"There they go!" she shouted as the van pulled away.

Faster and faster went the van, but Cruella's car drew closer and closer. She was screaming in anger. Then she began to yell in fear. Her car skidded on the icy road. Cruella tried to stop it, but her car spun around and slid into a ditch.

The last the Dalmatians saw of Cruella, she was standing beside her wrecked car having a nasty temper tantrum.

When the van reached the cozy little house in London, Roger and Anita were overjoyed. And when they counted the dogs, they discovered that they now had one hundred and one Dalmatians!

"We'll buy a big place in the country," said Roger. "We'll have a Dalmatian plantation!"

And they did exactly that. Pongo, Perdita, and all the spotted puppies lived there happily ever after.

WALT DISNEY'S
Alice in Wonderland

Alice was growing very tired, listening to her sister read. Just as her eyes began to close, she saw a white rabbit hurry by, looking at his pocket watch and talking to himself.

Alice thought that was very curious indeed—
a talking rabbit with a pocket watch! So she followed
him into a rabbit hole beneath a big tree.

And down she fell, down to the center of the
world, it seemed.

197

When Alice landed with a thump, the White
Rabbit was just disappearing through a door which
was much too small for her.

Alice drank from a bottle on the table and
shrank away to a very tiny size. But now she could
not reach the key to the little door!

At last Alice found a way to get through the
little door. Seated on a bottle, she floated into
Wonderland on a mysterious sea.

On through Wonderland Alice went,
looking for the White Rabbit. She met two jolly
fellows, Tweedle Dum and Tweedle Dee. They did
not know the Rabbit, so Alice hurried on.

At a neat little house in the woods,
at last she met the White Rabbit himself!

The Rabbit sent Alice into his little
house to hunt for his gloves. But instead she found
some cookies labeled Take One. So she did.

The cookie made Alice grow as big as the house. What a sight! Rabbit and his friend Dodo thought she was a dreadful monster.

Alice picked a carrot from Rabbit's garden.
Eating it made her small again, so small that she
was soon lost in a forest of grass.

Alice found herself in a garden of talking live flowers. There were bread-and-butterflies and rocking-horseflies, too.

Alice thought the garden was a pleasant place. But the flowers thought Alice was just a weed, so they would not let her stay.

Next Alice met a haughty Caterpillar blowing smoke rings. He told Alice to eat his mushroom if she wished to change her size.

Alice sampled one side, and shot up taller than the tree-tops, frightening the birds. But another bite made Alice just the right size.

"Now which way shall I go?" Alice wondered. The signposts she found along the path were no help—they pointed all over.

"If I were looking for the White Rabbit, I'd ask the Mad Hatter," said a grinning Cheshire Cat up in a tree. "He lives down there."

Alice found the Mad Hatter and the March Hare celebrating their un-birthdays at a tea party. She joined them for a while.

After that nonsensical tea party, Alice wanted to go home. But none of the strange creatures seemed to know the way.

Alice wandered into the Queen's Garden. Soon, along came the Royal Procession. And who should be the royal trumpeter but the White Rabbit himself!

The Queen of Hearts asked Alice to play croquet. But Alice did not like the looks of the game.

"Off with her head!" cried the Queen.

Away Alice ran, while the army of cards gave chase, down all the tangled paths of Wonderland, and back to the riverbank.

"I'm glad to be back where things are really what they seem," said Alice as she woke up from her strange Wonderland dream.